To
Anna

First published in 2005 in Great Britain by
Barrington Stoke Ltd, Sandeman House, Trunk's Close,
55 High Street, Edinburgh EH1 1SR
www.barringtonstoke.co.uk

ISBN 1-842993-30-5

Printed in Great Britain by Bell & Bain Ltd

Contents

Sally Mack

Just Another Saturday

Yeah. Just another Saturday.

That's what I thought.

I work for my Auntie Rena from 8 o'clock in the morning till 5 in the evening at her café, The Last Stop Caff.

I'm always run off my feet.

I'm as hot and sticky in my pink nylon overall as one of Auntie Rena's yum-yums.

I make coffee.

Tea.

1

I cut up cake.

I try not to cut my fingers.

Or lick the leftovers in public.

I serve sandwiches.

I wipe down tables.

I try not to trip over shopping bags.

But I trip over shopping bags.

I dish up soup.

I spill it ...

I'm so clumsy I always spill *something* ... over my hands. Down some woman's skirt. Over some bloke's lap ...

Soon as I *do* spill anything hot over someone, Auntie Rena comes rushing over to mop up the mess. She flaps and fusses.

"Oh, dearie me! Take a wee break, Sally," she tells me. She shoos me into the back kitchen.

If you heard how kind Auntie Rena's voice can sound you would think she was:

a. My real auntie. Not just some old pal of my mum's.

or

b. Not one *bit* angry with Sally Mack. Her big clumsy slave.

But Auntie Rena *is* always angry when I spill stuff. Fizzing. When she smiles and says, "Take a wee break," that's really secret code for, "SALLY MACK! YOU STUPID GREAT LUMP OF LARD ON LEGS! BE MORE CAREFUL OR YOU ARE **SACKED**."

As soon as Auntie Rena's looked after her burnt customer and given them a free meal to make up, she stomps into the back kitchen to give me grief.

"Sally Mack, this is your last warning," Auntie Rena nip, nip, nips.

Every Saturday.

After that, it's *Teach That Stupid Sally Mack A Lesson Time.*

Auntie Rena makes me clean out the caff's toilets. One of them's *always* blocked. All of them honk.

Yeah. Just another Saturday.

That's what I was thinking while I swished a toilet brush round the bowl in the Gents. Yuk! I was trying *not* to look at what I was trying to clean. I was also trying not to breathe. It was toxic in there.

Man, if only I could quit Auntie Rena's stupid job.

I'd just *love* to march out of the toilets and into the caff right now. I'd shove the dirty end of this toilet brush into Auntie Rena's hand. Pull off my pink nylon overall.

I'd give Auntie Rena a bit of grief for a change.

"Don't bother sacking me, 'cos I'm leaving. Don't need your stupid job any more," I'd say.

Then I'd walk out the caff with my head in the air. Into the sunset. Or better still, into the bus station next door. I'd buy a one-way ticket to Something Better Than This.

I'd do it. Right now. Make everything different. Better. If only I didn't need this stupid job so bad.

But I do.

I'm saving up to start my own business. Making punky funky cut-up T-shirts out of old clothes. I need a proper sewing machine for that. And I need Auntie Rena's stupid job to make the money to buy one.

Life's unfair that way. Unfair as Auntie Rena.

Because today I didn't even *do* a hot spill on that girl.

Her coffee went nowhere near her.

A few splashes landed on her lumpy great rucksack.

Which was waterproof.

Right away I said, "Sorry. Sorry, I'll wipe that off."

But that girl made such a blooming song and dance ...

"Idiot," she said, so stuck up and flipping **LOUD** I bet even Auntie Rena's deaf punters heard. Because *everyone* in the caff turned and stared at me. Then the girl's voice went all whiney.

"My bag's *soaked*," she moaned. "I can't sit on a bus to Manchester with a wet bag! Total DIS-A-STER! All my weekend clothes are in there. Ruined. Now I can't go to *Rock Out*. I've a free ticket and everything. You should lose your job for being so clumsy."

Sally Mack
Rucksack Girl

"Och, miss. Your lovely bag's soaked. That Sally Mack is the *worst* waitress I've ever had in my bistro ..."

Auntie Rena was *still* fussing round that girl. I'd finished cleaning the manky toilets and was back in the caff, behind the counter. I was thinking that Auntie Rena was thinking Rucksack Girl gave the caff class. She was trying to sound posh. How could she call her greasy spoon caff a bistro? If the Last Stop's a bistro then I'm J.Lo's clone!

Auntie Rena, you sound daft, I thought, and I wished I could do a runner.

I wished I could blag my way to *Rock Out*. Stuff this job. Then I could bliss out for two days at the biggest outdoor festival of the summer ...

But Auntie Rena saw me. "Sal *–lee*!!!" she shouted. She made me serve Rucksack Girl and her friends three mega milk floats. They come with sugar sprinkles and choccy flakes and cherries and gold straws. The nearest thing to posh in this caff.

"On the house for the young ladies now, Sally," said Auntie Rena. Still in her put-on posh voice. She made sure Rucksack Girl and her two mates could hear.

Bet they didn't hear what Auntie Rena growled at me in her normal pit-bull voice, "And I'll be docking nine quid for these out your pay, Sally Mack!"

No way! The crap dosh in this crap job was the only thing that kept me going. Now, thanks to some drama queen, I had to work my butt off for nine hours ... for next to nothing! I was *mad*. I frothed up milk, and I glared at Rucksack Girl who'd screwed me big-time. Just because of a few drops of coffee.

It looked like Rucksack Girl had forgotten all about the *Total DIS-A-STER* that was all my fault. She was too busy watching me instead. Her eyes tracked every single thing I did. It made me clumsy. I dropped a spoon with a clatter. Slopped milk all over my hands. Over the floor.

I saw Rucksack Girl nudge both her mates. She wanted them to stare at me too. Rucksack Girl's face was mean, even when she was laughing.

"Sal-*lee*!" Rucksack Girl sang higher, louder and sillier than Auntie Rena.

"Sal-*lee*!"

"Sal-*lee*! Milk floats on the house, Sal-*lee*," her mates started too. They sounded like three mad cats singing.

"Hey, if I was that waitress I'd change my name from Sal-*lee* to Plain Jane," one of Rucksack Girl's mates giggled. She flapped her hand towards me while I carried the milk floats across the caff.

9

"No, Pippa. I'd wear a bag on my head," hooted Rucksack Girl's other mate.

By now I was at Rucksack Girl's elbow. As I put the tray on her table, she looked me up and down. Down and up.

"If that waitress was me," Rucksack Girl snorted, "I'd just give up and *die*."

Rucksack Girl and her mates had loud fake voices. Everyone in the caff was turning round to look at them. Trying to hear what they were saying. The old people in the caff were staring at these three girls like they'd zoomed into the Last Stop on a spaceship. These girls weren't like anyone else who came into Auntie Rena's caff. They weren't wearing raincoats or zipped into old anoraks. They weren't loaded down with bags from Pricecutters. They didn't wear flat caps or hearing aids. None of them had curlers in like old Mrs McSween.

These girls weren't like me either. Rucksack Girl and her mates were blonde. Tanned. Glam. They wore tiny vests. Even if I sewed all their vests together, they wouldn't make one of my punky funky T-shirts. They texted into tiny mobiles. Only took one nibble from the big slabs of free cake Auntie Rena made me serve them. Then they pushed their plates away.

"This place *sucks*," said one of the blondes. She held her mobile up and took a picture of the oldies. Snap. Then she snapped me. She giggled.

"It's dire," her mate nodded. Her nose was scrunched up as if everyone in Auntie Rena's caff had farted at once.

"Totally," Rucksack Girl nodded to her mate. She was glaring at me.

"Let's scoot before we catch an ugly bug," she said, still glaring at me. Then she headed for the door.

"Let's go and buy some shoes. Mummy gave me piles of cash," Rucksack Girl said.

"Isn't the cash for *Rock Out*?" one blonde mate asked her.

"You've got your bus ticket to Manchester," said the other blonde.

"—and aren't you meeting your brother there?" the first blonde put in. She winked at Rucksack Girl. "Hey, think of all those *dishy* music guys Crispin works for!"

"And what about your Backstage Pass?" First blonde mate pointed at Rucksack Girl's rucksack. "You'll meet *everyone*."

Rucksack Girl gave a shrug. Then she pointed over to me and she stamped her foot so hard my tray rattled.

"How can I meet rock stars when I stink of coffee?" Rucksack Girl huffed. Then she flung open the caff door.

"Anyway, I feel like shopping now," she said, and with that, she tossed her head and marched outside.

"Instead of going to *Rock Out?*" her first blonde mate asked as she rushed out after Rucksack Girl.

"What about your bag?" called the second blonde. She had picked up the rucksack and was dragging it out of the caff.

"Get real, Pippa," Rucksack Girl's voice was high and loud. "I'm not carrying *that*

12

through town. Let sad Sal-*lee* bin it. It's full of last year's gear anyway. I was going to dump it at *Rock Out*," she said. And just before the door shut she kicked the rucksack back into the caff. It skidded across the floor towards me.

Who knows if Rucksack Girl aimed at me or not. All *I* know is I was leaning over old Mrs McSween when the bag hit my ankles.

Bullseye!

I stumbled.

Tripped.

And the plate of hot lentil soup I was carrying flew out my hands.

Auntie Rena wouldn't even let me wash the soup off my face.

"You're sacked, Sally Mack," she said with a snarl and she pushed a £20 note into my hand. Then she shoved me and Rucksack Girl's rucksack out of the caff.

Sally Mack

Inside the Rucksack ...

So there I was.

No job.

20 quid in one hand.

Rucksack Girl's rucksack in the other.

Lumpy lentil soup all over my pink nylon overall.

Must have looked a picture!

No way could I go public in this state. So I nipped into the bus station next to the caff to get sorted. Me and Rucksack Girl's rucksack. Man, it was heavy! That stuck-up cow must have thought you took rocks to a rock festival. The bag was so lumpy I couldn't pull it into the toilet with me.

I dragged it into the Mother and Baby room instead. I thought I'd dump it there.

But the first thing I did was peel off my vile pink overall. I threw it in the nappy bin.

"Missing you already!" I cheered and punched the air. Grinned into this big, long mirror.

"*I see you baby ...*" I started to sing. Then my grin drooped into an upside down horseshoe.

Man, look at the state of me!

I'll start with my hair. It's always a mess anyway. It sticks up and it sticks out. It's wild and frizzy and dirty yellow. That's apart from the bits dyed pink. And the bits dyed black. Now, thanks to Rucksack Girl, there were peas in it. Parsley growing out of the top. And chopped carrots.

There was carrot everywhere, in fact. Clumps of carrot were squished between the laces of my Vans. There were little mushy orange jewels – or rather shiny carrot blobs – all down my only good jeans. The carrot was stuck on with big globs of lentil glue.

Look at you! I even had to slag *myself* off while I washed my hair out in the Mother and Baby sink. The only bit of my body that was soup-free was my T-shirt. Lucky. Because I was wearing my coolest one. The first one I ever made. The one that made me want to make lots of punky funky cut-up T-shirts for a living. It was the best-looking thing about me, if you must know.

That T-shirt fits me like a second skin. It's made up of logos from all my favourite bands: *Sex Pistols, Blondie, The Clash, Iggy Pop, Patti Smith, New York Dolls, Ramones*, of course ... I cut them all off other T-shirts and sewed the bits together.

I always wore that T-shirt to work on Saturdays under the sweaty pink nylon overall. It made me feel as if the *real* Sally Mack was still in there. Under the pink nylon. She might just burst out one of these days ...

"Huh, the real Sally Mack. Total sad-sack," I said to myself in the mirror. I needed to clean up, sort myself out. Go and get another job. But I didn't know where to begin. So I slumped down against a wall to think.
I plonked my butt down on Rucksack Girl's rucksack.

A bag full of old gear, she'd said. *She was going to dump it at Rock Out.*

A bag she threw at me.

A bag that lost me my job.

A bag she didn't want.

Honest. When I peeked inside that rucksack I was only looking for something clean to wear home.

And I only unpacked Rucksack Girl's ...

earplugs,

four Pot Noodles,

travel kettle,

travel iron,

hair tongs,

two bog rolls,

17

Dettox spray

wet wipes

cuddly toy (honest!)

brand new sleeping bag

four lace thongs

and the fullest make-up bag I've ever seen ...

because I needed clean, dry clothes.

At the bottom of the bag I *did* find jeans. Diesel – two pairs. Both a tight fit but way less tatty than the ones I had on. There was a denim jacket to match. Looked ace over my T-shirt. Rock chick ace. There were shoes too. Fancy cowboy boots, not worn Vans. The boots had pointy toes that would squish my big wide feet. And heels.

But hey, I thought, *they'll do fine for walking home in.*

That's what I planned to do next.

After this suck of a Saturday.

But then I saw the envelope. It was stuffed in the side pocket of the rucksack.

It said *SALLY!!!* in bright, happy letters.

Like it was just for me.

"'Cos I'm the only Sally round here, right?" I said as I ripped open the envelope.

Wrong.

Inside the envelope, there was a free ticket to *Rock Out* and an **ACCESS ALL AREAS** Backstage Pass.

The **ACCESS ALL AREAS** Backstage Pass was made out ... not to me, Sally Mack. But to a **MS SALLY PARK**.

Rucksack Girl.

I had to laugh.

"Hey, **MS SALLY PARK**. We've got something in common after all," I said as I let my finger run along the Backstage Pass. The pass hung on a red string. I slipped it over my head. Let it dangle over my punky-funky T-shirt.

"Now, let's see what else is in here," I said. There was a note scribbled inside the envelope too.

Have a blast, sis.

See you in the dance tent!

CRISPIN

the note said.

"Sorry, *Crispin!* I don't think I'll be dancing with you. Not if you're anything like your stuck-up sister," I said. I chucked the note in the nappy bin.

After that I had a look in Sally Park's big fat make-up bag. I ran her red lip gloss round and round my big wide grin. But I had to be quick.

You see, there was a bus to Manchester going in ten minutes. There was a ticket for the bus in the envelope.

And guess what?

The new Ms Sally Park would be on that bus.

Keith Scully

Who Cares?

You know how it feels when you've been looking forward to something for ages, and when it's there at last, it doesn't seem so great? Well, that's how I felt. That's how my Saturday started out.

My name's Keith Scully by the way.

I was feeling OK when I left home in the morning. I wouldn't say I was feeling *fantastic* or anything, but I was doing OK. The sun was shining, my rucksack was packed, and I was off to Manchester to see the best band in the world – the *Dead Holes*. What could be better?

Plus there'd be no parents, no teachers, no rules. No grief. Just me and my two best mates – Danny and James – and a long weekend of music and madness.

Perfect.

I was even feeling pretty good about the way that I looked. My white leather jacket was perfectly dirty, my hair was a perfect mess, and my spots had chosen the perfect time to disappear.

Too good to be true?

Of *course* it was too good to be true. It always is.

It began to go wrong as soon as I got to the train station. For a start, it was crowded with football fans. There were hundreds of them. They were all over the station, shouting and chanting and drinking. I wasn't really scared of them. But I'm not stupid. I know what some people think when they see a kid in a white leather jacket which is covered in badges and patches and studs.

Some people think – *Hey, let's beat the crap out of him.* So, as I walked over to the station clock, I kept my head down.

I was supposed to be meeting Danny and James there. 12 o'clock, we'd said. At 10 past 12 there was still no sign of them anywhere. And the train to Manchester was leaving in 20 minutes. I'd already bought the tickets and booked our seats.

"You get the tickets", James had told me, "and we'll pay you back – OK?"

"Yeah, but—"

"What?" James asked.

"Well, I already bought the *Rock Out* tickets ..."

"Yeah, and we're paying you back for them. What's the problem?"

"Nothing—"

"I mean, if it's too much trouble ..." James said.

"No," I'd told him, "no, it's all right. There's no problem".

23

So there I was, Mr No Problem, on my own under the station clock, waiting for Danny and James and trying to look as if everything was OK. I kept looking at the train tickets and reading what it said on them. For about the 127th time I read, *Coach C, Seats 22A, 22B, and 23A.*

The loudspeaker said the train was there now, on Platform 5. People were starting to go through the gates. I was beginning to feel pretty stupid.

I rang James on my mobile, and he answered after a bit.

"Yeah?" he said.

I couldn't hear him very well. I could hear the TV in the background. The volume must have been up loud. All around me in the station, the football fans were chanting their heads off – *COME ON YOU GOONERS ... AARRRSENOWUUUU ... AARRRSENOWUUUU ... AARRRSENOWUUUU ...*

"James?" I shouted. "It's Keith here."

"What?" James shouted back.

"It's Keith."

"Who?" James couldn't hear me either.

"Keith – Keith Scully."

"Hey, Scully—"

"Where are you? The train's just about to go."

"What train?" James asked.

"The train to Manchester—"

"Manchester? Oh, right ... Manchester. Yeah, the *Rock Out* thing. Right. Yeah, we were going to ring you about that."

"What?" I yelled.

"We were going to ring you," James went on.

"What do you mean?"

He didn't answer. I knew he'd put his hand over his phone and now he was talking to someone else. I couldn't make out what he was saying, but I heard him say my name. Then I thought I heard someone trying not to laugh out loud. That sounded like Danny.

"Scully?" James said into the phone. "You still there?"

"Yeah – what's going on?"

"Nothing – we can't make it, that's all."

I heard Danny shout over to him – "Tell Scully something's come up."

James laughed. This time he didn't cover up the phone. "You *wish*," he said to Danny. Danny laughed again.

"Sorry," James said to me. "It's just that we met these girls yesterday, and they want to see us again tonight."

"What girls?"

"They're hot, man. I mean, *really* hot. They're too good to turn down."

"Yeah, but the festival—"

"Sorry, mate. Maybe some other time – yeah?"

"But what about the tickets—?" I started to say, but James wasn't listening any more. He'd covered the phone again and he was talking to Danny. I could hear them. I couldn't make out what they were saying but they were laughing. In the background I could hear the TV. Cat Deeley was having a laugh and talking to the boys from *Westlife*.

Westlife?

Westlife?

Shit.

Who cares?

I put away my mobile, picked up my rucksack and headed off for the train.

Who cares? I kept telling myself as I walked along the platform. *Who cares if they're not coming? Not me. Why should I care? If they want to sit at home watching Westlife on CD:UK, well that's up to them, isn't it? If they want to spend the night with a couple of hot girls instead of spending the night with me ...*

Who cares?

I was kidding myself, of course. I knew deep down that I *did* care. Just like I knew that Danny and James weren't my best mates. Never had been. Never would be. Never in a million years. We didn't even *like* each other, to tell you the truth. We had nothing in common. They didn't even like the same music. I'm not even sure they *liked* music. They probably didn't even know what *Rock Out* was. When I'd talked about getting tickets, they just thought it was something to do on a Saturday night if there was nothing else going on.

I *knew* that.

I'd known it all along.

So why did I care?

I couldn't be bothered to work out why.

It was all too much right now.

I opened the door and got on just in time. The train began to pull out of the station.

Keith Scully

Thugs

The train was full of people. There were
football fans in there too and they were
really noisy. It took me ages to make my way
along the crowded carriages to Coach C.
When I did get there I found myself
surrounded by the three scariest thugs in the
world.

Thug One was enormous – a huge great
bear of a man. He had a big fat head and a
big fat neck and a big fat belly that rolled
over the edge of the table in front of him.
Next to him, Thug Two, had grey skin and

sunken eyes and on his neck were tattoos of skulls and hammers. Thug Three was the whitest person I've ever seen. White skin, white hair, white T-shirt and jeans.

There were beer cans all over the table and carrier bags full of bottles on the floor. I was all on my own, sitting there and looking around like an idiot. The carriage went quiet. The three thugs were looking hard at me.

"What you looking at?" the big one grunted.

"Sorry?" I said.

"You want something?"

"No," I muttered. I tried to smile, "No, I was just …"

"What?"

"Nothing," I said.

Some other fans in the next carriage had started singing again. Along with the football chant they were smacking their hands on the windows. It sounded primitive and wild and scary.

"Nice jacket," the thug with the tattoos said to me.

"What?"

He bent across the table and grinned into my face. His breath stank of beer and his teeth were yellow and crooked. My heart sank.

The nightmare had just begun.

What's your name? he hissed.

Keith, yeah? Keith what?

Smelly?

Oh, Scully – I thought you said Smelly. Hur hur hur. Where you going, Keith?

Cock Out? What's that – a gay festival? Hur hur hur. Is that why you're wearing that poofy white jacket?

Here, have a beer.

What d'you mean – you don't like beer? Everyone likes beer. Go on, Keithy-boy, drink it.

What's all them badges about, then? They pictures of your boyfriends?

No? The what Holes? Dead Holes? They a gay band?

Who's that one, then?

Who?

Kiefer who? Nah, never heard of him. Hey, look, he's got a poofy white jacket just like yours ... you fancy him or something? Only joking. Hur hur hur.

Come on, Keith, you're not drinking your beer ...

You like football?

Yeah? Who d'you support?

What d'you mean – no-one?

Come on, Keith, you're not singing ...

AARRRSENOWUUUU ... AARRRSENOWUUUU ... AARRRSENOWUUUU ...

Here, drink up, have another beer.

Hey, Keith – does your mum know you're a poof?

Hur hur hur

Hur hur hur ...

Hur hur hur hur hur hur hur ...

When, at long last, I got off the train I was:

1) a bit drunk.

2) totally fed up.

And 3) beginning to think that perhaps I *was* gay.

Keith Scully

Stopping too Soon

Was I gay? I *was* a bit drunk and totally fed up, but I couldn't work out if I was gay or not. Did it matter? I mean, there's nothing wrong with being gay. It's just that I'm not. Never have been. Never will be, as far as I know.

All those stupid jokes on the train, all that stuff about my white leather jacket and my badges and boyfriends and poofs ... They'd just made me feel odd about myself.

I knew it didn't matter if I was gay. But, even so, just like not knowing if Danny and

James *were* my friends, I wished it didn't bother me so much.

At least the train journey from hell was over now. The thugs were heading off to their football match and I was heading off to find the *Rock Out* buses that went from the station to the festival.

I *wasn't* gay.

My jacket *wasn't* poofy.

The badges on it weren't pictures of my boyfriends. They were just pictures of the *Dead Holes*. I didn't fancy Kiefer Shelley. It's just most of the badges were pictures of him. He was my favourite *Dead Hole*. I liked the way he played the guitar. Yeah, OK – so his name was a bit like mine, and he wore a white leather jacket like mine ...

But that's all there was to it.

The buses were at the end of the station car park by a cardboard sign that said *Rock Out – Buses*. There were three buses and the first two were already full. I had to get on the last one – which was totally empty. As soon as I got on, the driver shut the doors and started the engine. The bus began to move away from the station. The driver was a little man with a dirty white beard and glassy eyes. He had a pipe stuck in the corner of his mouth but he hadn't lit it yet. On his head was a black leather motorcycle cap. He looked like a mental goblin.

"Aren't we waiting for anyone else, then?" I asked him.

"No," he muttered. "You gotta sit down."

I went right to the back of the bus and sat down.

All alone.

It felt kind of weird. On the train, 20 minutes ago, I'd wanted so badly to be on my own. Now that I *was* on my own, I needed someone to talk to.

After the bus had been going for about 10 minutes, I began to feel a bit better. I wasn't sure how far it was to the festival, but we'd already passed a few traffic signs with arrows pointing to *Rock Out*. *We must be near*, I thought.

10 minutes, 15 minutes ... whatever.

I'd be there in plenty of time to see the *Dead Holes*. No trouble. Get myself right down the front, right next to the speakers, get those guitars blasting right through my head.

Nothing to think about.

Nothing to worry about.

It was all going to be OK.

Nothing could go wrong now ...

Unless the bus broke down.

It happened without any warning. One minute we were rattling along – the engine was juddering, the windows shaking – and then suddenly everything just stopped. The engine died, everything fell silent, and the bus just slid to the side of the road and stopped dead.

I sat there for a minute. I waited for the bus to get going again, but nothing happened. I looked out of the window. We were on a long, straight road in the middle of nowhere.

There were no pavements, just steep grass banks on both sides of the road.

Great, I thought.

I got up and walked to the front of the bus. The driver was just sitting there, sucking on his pipe.

"What's the matter?" I asked him. "Why have we stopped?"

"Uh uh," he grunted. "I told 'em – it needs fixing. I told 'em."

"What?"

"These old buses," he went on, "they ain't no good in the rain. Engine gets wet. I told 'em."

I looked out of the window again. It wasn't raining. It hadn't been raining all day.

"What are we going to do?" I said.

"Nothing," he said with a shrug. "Wait for the tow-truck."

"How long will that be?"

"Hour ... maybe two. Truck's gotta come from the depot."

"Two *hours?*"

He looked back at me. "Truck's gotta come from the depot."

I couldn't wait two hours. If I waited two hours I'd miss the *Dead Holes*. I couldn't spend another two hours with this grunting little goblin man. I'd go mad.

"How far is it to the festival?" I asked him.

"What – walking?"

No, flying – I thought.

"Yeah – walking," I said.

"Uh uh," he said. He still had his pipe in his mouth. "Not far – about a mile."

"Which way?"

He took his pipe out of his mouth and tapped it on the windscreen in front of him. "Straight up there," he said. "Just keep going along this road – you can't miss it. Just follow the traffic until you get to a ..."

I didn't wait to hear the rest of it.

Keith Scully
All Change

Before I tell you what happened next, you need to know a few things.

Firstly – I didn't like Kiefer Shelley *because* his name sounded a bit like mine, or *because* he wore a white leather jacket like mine. No, I liked him because he was in the *Dead Holes*, and the *Dead Holes* were a brilliant band, and he was a brilliant guitarist.

Secondly – I was wearing my white leather jacket long before Kiefer came along with his.

40

I've had mine for years. So it wasn't like I was copying him or anything – OK?

And thirdly – I liked the *Dead Holes* because they were loud and nasty and my parents didn't like them. I liked them because they had attitude. I liked them because they rocked.

That's what I thought, anyway. What happened next made me see just how wrong you can be sometimes. You think you know all about a band but you don't.

OK, so what happened next was this. I'd been walking along the road for about 5 minutes. At last I was close to the festival site. I could just about see it in the distance – lots of big tents, crowds of people, stage lights and flags and trucks full of gear. I could hear it, too. I could hear the boom of the music far away, even if I couldn't make out the songs yet. Drums, guitars, thumping bass. It sounded really exciting. Thrilling.

I started to walk faster.

There was a lot of traffic on the narrow road, all going to the festival. Because there weren't any pavements it wasn't that easy to walk. I had to keep in close to the side of the road, out of the way of all the cars rushing past. If I moved too far to the side, I'd end up falling down the steep grass banks into the fields below. It was muddy down there. And full of nettles. And brambles. And cow shit.

And I was still feeling a little bit drunk.

So I was walking carefully.

Watching my step.

Trying to keep calm.

Trying to ignore the *whoosh-whoosh-whoosh* of the traffic ripping past me. Sometimes the cars were so close they nearly touched me. I tried not to think what would happen if I took half a step to the right, into the road. I tried not to think about being squashed flat with my white leather jacket flapping in the wind like the wing feathers of a dead seagull.

I thought I was doing OK.

I was getting there. One step at a time ...

I was getting there. I was doing fine.

And then it happened.

As the traffic went on roaring past, something soft and heavy suddenly slammed into my back. It knocked me off my feet. The next thing I knew I was tumbling head over heels down the grass bank, and the world was turning upside down.

It seemed to take a long time to get to the bottom of the bank. I just kept falling and rolling, then sliding on my back for a while, then rolling again. I was grunting and groaning and spitting and cursing as I fell. And then, at last, I crashed into a thick bramble hedge and landed with a thump in a ditch full of cow shit.

I lay there for a while not moving. I was trying to get some air into my lungs, and then I sat up slowly to check myself over. I seemed to be all right. Nothing was broken. I was badly out of breath and I was cut and scratched. My clothes were all ripped and covered in crap.

But apart from that I was fine.

Terrific.

Yeah, never felt better.

I looked around. Where was I now? And
what the hell had hit me? Then I saw it.
A bag – a black holdall – was lying in the mud
beside the ditch. *That's* what had hit me.
That's what had knocked me off my feet.
A black holdall. Someone must have thrown
it out of a car as they were driving past me.
But why? Why would anyone throw a
perfectly good holdall out of a car?

As I was sitting there thinking about it, I
heard people talking on the road above me.
I thought at first that someone must have
seen what happened to me and had stopped to
see if I was all right. I crawled over to the
bramble hedge and looked up at the side of
the road. It wasn't just *someone*. I couldn't
believe who I was looking up at ...

It was the *Dead Holes*.

They were in a jet-black minibus with
tinted windows. The front windows were
wound down, and I could see Dane (the singer)
and John (the bass player) sitting in the front
seat next to the driver. I didn't know who the
driver was, and I couldn't see Pete (the
drummer) anywhere, but Kiefer Shelley was
there ...

44

He was right there!

He wasn't inside the minibus. He was standing at the side of the road, looking down into the field ... I couldn't believe it!

Kiefer Shelley!

Was I dreaming? Was I going to be rescued by the *Dead Holes*?

I grabbed the holdall and was just about to start clambering back up the bank, when I heard Dane say something.

"... and why d'you throw your bloody bag out of the window anyway?" he was shouting to Kiefer. "What's the matter with you?"

"I didn't *mean* to throw it out of the window, did I?" Kiefer told him. "I was aiming it at your head."

"Oh, right – so it's *my* fault, is it? It's my fault you've lost your poxy bag."

"I didn't say that, did I? And, anyway, what do *you* care? You're the one who said my jacket sucked. What do you care if I chuck it out the window?"

"I *don't* care. We're late. Get back in the car."

"No, I want my jacket ..."

They carried on arguing and I edged back behind the brambles and ducked down out of sight. I needed time to think. My head was suddenly racing with lots of weird information.

Firstly – I was lying at the bottom of a grass bank in the middle of nowhere because Kiefer Shelley had thrown his bag out of the *Dead Holes'* minibus. How weird was *that?*

Secondly – either they didn't know that the bag had hit me, or they simply didn't care.

Thirdly – they didn't sound like a band with *attitude*, they sounded like a bunch of ten-year-old kids. They sounded like wimps. Spoiled brats. Tossers.

Fourthly – from what I could see, they weren't dressed anything like the *Dead Holes* that I knew. The *Dead Holes* that I knew wore ripped jeans and leather – they didn't wear comfy sweatshirts and nice clean trousers.

And last of all – the *Dead Holes* that I knew didn't have posh voices. They had rough, tough cockney accents. But the *Dead Holes* I was looking at on the road had very posh voices.

It wasn't just weird, it was *pathetic*.

I could hear John, the bass player. He was talking now. He sounded even posher than the rest of them.

"Oh, come on, Kiefer," he was saying, "just leave it. It's filthy down there. Look at all that dirty mud and everything. It's only a jacket, isn't it? You've got plenty more, haven't you?"

"Yeah, loads ..."

"Was there anything else in the bag?"

"Not really ..."

"So *leave* it. Let some poor little sod find it. It'll make their sad little day. Come on, Kief, let's go. The sooner we get this gig done, the sooner we can get out of here."

I didn't really know what I was feeling as I watched Kiefer turn around. He looked as if he was in a real sulk as he walked back to the minibus. I was angry, fed up, sick. I felt let down. I felt betrayed. How stupid was I? I'd thought the *Dead Holes* were really cool, when in fact they were just a bunch of fakes.

Kiefer had got back into the minibus now. The tinted windows had closed. I heard the engine start up, and then the minibus drove off down the road.

"*Dead Holes?*" I mumbled to myself as I opened up Kiefer's holdall. "*Dead Holes?* Yeah, right – bloody *Arse Holes*, more like. All of them."

I pulled Kiefer's white leather jacket out of the bag. He'd said he had loads of them ... maybe this one didn't mean *anything* to him. It was just another jacket. Just one of his *many* white leather jackets. Jackets he only wore anyway when he was on stage.

Yeah, well, I said to myself, *if he doesn't want it ...*

I took off my shit-covered jacket and tried on Kiefer's.

Perfect fit.

I was still feeling angry as I dug into the bag again. I was beginning to feel something else, too. The bag wasn't empty. There was loads of stuff in there – a pair of expensive ripped jeans, a leather belt with a brass buckle, some leather wrist bands, a necklace, a brand-new pair of £200 trainers ...

I couldn't help smiling to myself.

I crouched down behind the bramble hedge and tried everything on.

Apart from the trainers – which were a couple of sizes too small – everything else was a perfect fit. I threw the trainers away. I took everything out of the pockets of my dirty old clothes. Then I shoved the old clothes into Kiefer's bag. After that I put all the stuff from my old pockets into the lovely, clean, new pockets of my new clothes.

And that's when I found the Backstage Pass.

It was in one of the pockets of the white leather jacket, all folded up neatly in a see-through envelope. And it wasn't just any old Backstage Pass. It was an important, personal Backstage Pass.

PERFORMER, it said.

KIEFER SHELLEY, it said.

ACCESS ALL AREAS, it said.

"That'll do for me," I said.

I took the pass out of the envelope, shook out the red string and put it round my neck.

Then I headed off to the festival.

Sally Mack
Just One of the Crowd

Here I was. I'd been on the bus for 4 hours and Auntie Rena was far away now. I was at *Rock Out.*

At last!

The bus journey had been hot, sticky and boring. Just like everyone crammed onto the bus, I was desperate, and not just for a pee. I *had* to get into *Rock Out.*

I could hear music already.

Feel it.

Drumbeats under my feet were rippling the floor of the bus.

Jerky reggae riffs were making my pulse run faster.

Guitar sounds were swirling and soaring and wailing and waa-waaing ...

I just had to get off that bus.

Get into the music.

But it wasn't that easy.

Because outside the massive gates to the festival there were *crowds* of people. When I stepped off the bus I stepped into a sea of bodies and rucksacks and tents and coolboxes and guitars and babies in slings and punks and rockers and hippies and moshers and Goths and stoners and spotty herberts ... And they carried me along as if I was being pushed forward by one huge, smelly, sweaty wave.

And it was a NIGHTMARE.

I felt like yelling out.

You see, I could hear someone chanting, *Hey ho, let's go! Hey ho, let's go*! That was from the chorus of my favourite Ramones song. Hearing it was torture! It meant there was a good tribute band in there, on the other side of the gates. And I was stuck out here.

"Gimme me a break. I lost my job today. Let me in to *Rock Out*," I groaned. In my hand was Sally Park's ACCESS ALL AREAS Pass. I gripped onto it. Stared at it. Wished for a miracle ...

I must have wished pretty hard. Just then people started to move out of the way and let me pass. That square of cardboard on the red string round my neck did the trick.

One moment I was squashed up between a skinhead and a biker, squished thinner than Nicole Kidman.

The next moment ...

This bouncer walked up. He looked like he was made out of black concrete. He was a *giant* and he wore the biggest T-shirt I've ever seen. It had ROCK STEADY written over it. Giant ROCK STEADY pointed at my ACCESS ALL AREAS Pass and said, "Let the lady through. She's a VIP." His voice boomed over the crowd like God in some old movie.

By the way, the "lady" Giant ROCK STEADY was talking about was *me*.

Sally Mack
Faking It

"May I?" said Giant ROCK STEADY. He slung Rucksack Sally's rucksack onto his back as if it was empty. Then he helped me make my way to a gate marked **VIPs**. And, get this – on the other side of the gate there was a *red* carpet. It led down a private tunnel into the festival.

In front of me was a skinny guy in the *whitest* leather jacket I've ever seen. He strutted down the carpet like he was really something.

I waited for White Leather Jacket to flash his pass at another ROCK STEADY giant. Everyone else waiting to get into *Rock Out* round the main gates was looking over. It wasn't only White Leather Jacket they were gawping at. I could hear what some of them were saying:

He's in that band ...

Whassit called? ...

And I know her.

She's someone ...

Check her hair.

Love her T-shirt.

And he's GOR-geous!!!

But she's quite fat, isn't she ...?

Can you believe it? There were people taking pictures. Of White Leather Jacket. Of *me*!

White Leather Jacket had to be a proper VIP. I was looking hard at all his gear. The jeans he was wearing must have cost a mint – they had so many slashes in them. The jacket itself was so white you needed sunglasses to look at it. It was short. Skin tight. Nipped in at the waist. Girly. Only a huge star could walk around in *that*. White Leather Jacket walked the walk of a celeb, too. His walk was a bit of a Robbie Williams strut mixed with that Liam Gallagher gorilla-in-a-huff mooch. Plus he'd skinny Mick Jagger rock star legs and no bum. He was carrying a flash black holdall. He *had* to be a VIP.

Except for his shoes. They just *didn't* fit.

White Leather Jacket wore scruffy VANS. Same as the ones I'd dumped at the bus station. Only tattier.

Maybe he wanted to look right-on rock'n'roll, wearing something really old. Or maybe he had bunions on his feet and needed big wide shoes, same as me.

He walked off, down the tunnel, a proper VIP.

Not like me, Sally Mack.

I was just *Faking It*. Same as that TV show where you pretend to be someone

you're not. It was only Sally Park's ACCESS
ALL AREAS Pass that turned me into a VIP.

But, hey ho, I was getting away with it so
far.

"Welcome, Miss Park, food tent on your
left. Enjoy now!" Giant ROCK STEADY said.
He gave me back my rucksack and pointed
down the tunnel.

"Thanks," I said. Could he hear my
stomach rumbling? I was so hungry my legs
were wobbly. All I'd eaten in the last four
hours was a stick of Juicy Fruit and two of my
fingernails. The thought of free food must
have made my head spin because I turned and
waved before I went through the tunnel. Not
just at Giant ROCK STEADY. I waved at all
the crowds.

And guess what?

Everyone waved back.

"You're great," someone shouted out.

And I knew that meant crap-all. What's
great about someone just because they're on
a red carpet and you're not? But I dunno.
Hearing someone say something *good* about

me for a change ... it went to my head faster than voddy and Red Bull.

And a voice inside me said, *Go for it, Sally. Kid on you really are someone. Fake it, girl!*

So I did.

I put a swagger in my step. I tried to copy White Leather Jacket. Swung my arms like his. Tried to walk the walk.

"Here I am – Sally Park. Fashion queen. Stylist to the stars," I whispered. And I turned to give the crowd one last dazzling VIP smile, spinning round in Sally Park's high-heeled cowboy boots.

Big mistake.

I was doing far too many things at once. Faking it. Smiling. Carrying that huge rucksack. Swaggering. Swinging my arms. Humming to *Rockaway Beach*. Making fancy moves in heels I could hardly walk in. On hungry legs ...

No wonder I tripped.

I've always been clumsy – but what happened next was epic, even for me.

The cowboy boots spun me too fast. Wheeeeeee!

I lost my balance.

I swung round so fast my rucksack went flying off my back ...

Through the air it flew ...

Whoaaaa!!!!

... and thumped into White Leather Jacket guy's back.

Hard.

At the same moment my feet went from under me. I fell forward along the red carpet and into the tunnel. I was the second thing to hit White Leather Jacket.

It wasn't graceful. It wasn't pretty.

Poor White Leather Jacket didn't stand a chance.

His holdall went one way and he went the other. And I landed slap bang on top of him.

Lucky there was a carpet to break his fall.

At first I thought I'd killed him. I swear he wasn't breathing. He just lay underneath me. Very still. His eyes were closed. His face was *nearly* as white as his jacket. A *brand new* jacket. It had an Armani label still tied to the zip.

Damn! I thought.

I was trying to roll off him but I couldn't get away. White Leather Jacket's ACCESS ALL AREAS Pass had got tangled up with mine. We were stuck together. Me squashing the poor guy flat.

"Really sorry about this ... er ... Kiefer," I said. I tried to read the name on White Leather Jacket's pass as I untangled it. Then I read what was written underneath the name.

PERFORMER it said.

KIEFER SHELLEY.

PERFORMER.

Hell! This guy *was* a proper rock star. I hadn't heard of him – he was too young and pretty for me – but he was a rock star all the same.

"*And* he's dead," I said with a gulp.
I pushed aside about ten leather wrist thongs
as I tried to find his pulse. What if this
Kiefer guy was some megastar? Rockstars die
from drugs or booze or fast cars or dodgy
amps. They choke on their vomit. They don't
die when some big clumsy zero like me, with
a fake VIP pass, squashes them flat.

Even if he was dead, Kiefer Shelley was
cute. He'd thick dark hair, messed up just the
way I like a bloke's hair messed up. Sweet
mouth. Long, curling eyelashes ... and so
cute.

This was not good. If Kiefer Shelley was a
dead star because of me, then I was as good
as dead too. His girl fans would kill me. *And
his boy fans too*, I thought, as I looked even
closer at him. Anyone *that* cute, with a
jacket *that* white, *that* soft, plus a stupid
dreamcatcher necklace, *had* to like girls *and*
boys.

"Shit!" I was starting to panic. Kiefer
Shelley still hadn't moved. Should I give him
the Kiss of Life?

It was tempting. *Very* tempting.

It wasn't every day Sally Mack got to pin down a cute, helpless Rock Star. But what if Kiefer woke up while I was tickling his tonsils?

He'd die of shock. Or sue me.

I decided not to snog him. I shouted, "HELP!" instead.

But no-one heard me yell.

No wonder.

Because just as I yelled, "HELP!" this RACKET started up.

Jeez!

It was liquid pain. The singer couldn't sing. The guitars were out of tune. The drummer had no rhythm. The song was rubbish. And loud enough to wake the dead.

Really, *really* wake the dead.

Sally Mack

Kiefer Shelley Comes Back to Life

I'm not kidding – that racket really did wake the dead. Kiefer Shelley shot up like he'd had an electric shock. He knocked me onto my back. Now *I* was squashed flat.

"*Dead Holes!*" Kiefer shouted into my face. His breath honked a bit of stale beer, but he wasn't dead. In fact, he was very much alive. When he found *me* lying under him, he got up so fast he must have set a new world record for Jumping off an Ugly Bird. He looked a bit sick. He was breathing too fast.

I shouted at him, "No, you're not in a Dead Hole. You're alive. At *Rock Out*. Your name is KIEFER SHELLEY and I tripped you up. Keep still." It was hard to yell over the noise of the worst band I'd ever heard. But Kiefer Shelley sprang up into the air.

"*Dead Holes, Dead Holes. Anthem for Hate*," he chanted.

Then he ran on, out of the tunnel. Towards the noise. He was unsteady on his feet. His eyes were glassy. He was yelling the same words as the bloke shouting his head off on the nearest stage. All this pish about stabbing and dying in pain.

Jeez, Sally Mack, I thought to myself, *you were lucky you missed watching these bampots singing on TV.* Not that the bloke at the front of the stage *was* singing. He was just *screaming* into his mike in a really bad cockney accent like something was pissing him off. Sounded like Prince William doing Punk. He was dressed like Prince William, too, in a smart rugby shirt and pressed chinos.

Poor Kiefer Shelley. I was worried. What if I'd given him concussion? What was he on about – jibbering away about *Dead Holes*? Then running off. He shouldn't be going near that ugly noise. He should be somewhere calm. Someone should be looking after him ...

"Hey, Kiefer! Someone needs to look after you," I shouted.

I scooped up his holdall and my rucksack and went after his white leather jacket. That bit was easy. It was so bright and white you couldn't miss it. But it was hard to fight my way through the zillions of spotty herberts. They were all singing along in angry cockney accents to the worst band in the world. Plus I had one broken heel and two lots of luggage.

I found Kiefer at last. Poor guy was in a bad way. He was right at the front of the crowd. Pressed up to the stage. He was on his knees. His eyes were shut. He was rolling his head round and round. And – oh dear – he was playing air guitar.

No wonder everyone nearby was staring at Kiefer. Pointing at him. Laughing. Two guys even tried to shove him onto the stage.

I didn't mess about.

"Let's get you out of here, Kiefer," I shouted. I battered the spotty herberts out of the way with the holdall and my rucksack.

"He's sick, you creeps," I hissed. Then I pulled Kiefer away from that horrible, *horrible* singing.

I was firm with him. It's lucky that I'm strong, because poor Kiefer didn't want me to help him. He fought me all the way. Called me things I'm not going to say here. Gave me a dead leg. That hurt like hell. I knew it was all my fault. I'd knocked him out. From watching *ER* and *Casualty* I know a thump on the head can make you aggressive – you fight anyone who comes your way. So I just held tight to Kiefer's white leather sleeve and dragged him towards the VIP Food and Drink tent.

"Now, let me sit you somewhere quiet. Make sure you know where you are. Keep you awake for the next 24 hours," I promised

Kiefer. The two ROCK STEADY bouncers waved us into the VIP tent.

"Good luck going solo, Mr Shelley," the first one said when he saw Kiefer.

"He'll need more than luck. What a tosser! Zero talent," I think the second ROCK STEADY giant muttered to the first as I pulled Kiefer into the tent.

"Hur hur hur. Going for ugly now he's left the band," chuckled the first ROCK STEADY bloke. "Musta dug her out the bottom of a Dead Hole."

Ouch! I thought. *Who were they slagging off?* I turned to double-check that there wasn't some other VIP behind me. But they *did* mean me. I started to feel weak, a bit faint. Maybe it was because I'd turned round so fast. Or maybe I was just hungry.

For a moment I let go of Kiefer. That's when he took his chance and yanked away from me.

It was pretty dark in the VIP tent. Busy. And very hot. There were all these fat blokes in suits. They were standing around drinking wine and smoking cigars. Looked like they should be working in a bank, not hanging out at a summer rock festival.

There was only one person I could see who looked like a rock and roll VIP. He wore ripped jeans and a white leather jacket. He'd a bottle of beer in each hand and he was standing in front of this table that was piled with food.

There were curries and cakes and kebabs and sandwiches, puddings and pastas and nibbles and nuts. What a scoff! It was making my belly howl.

Kiefer Shelley was nodding to a waiter, "I'll have some of that. More of that. *Plenty* of that." His voice went all funny and swimmy inside my head as I watched his plate pile up. I felt myself moving like a zombie towards the table and all that food.

"Good. Y'mus be feeling betta—" I started to say to Kiefer.

But then my legs gave way for the second time that day.

Keith Scully
Catching a Crazy Girl

You know how it feels when you wake up
from a dream. Everything is suddenly real
again, but you don't know what's going on.
And you don't know where you are. You know
you're not dreaming any more, but it still
feels like you are.

Well that's how I felt in the VIP tent.
When I turned around and saw this crazy-
looking girl wobbling around in front of me.
I felt weird. Like all those things I just said.

My head felt odd, as if I'd just been knocked out or something. I didn't know where I was. I wasn't even sure *who* I was for a minute. I couldn't remember my name – Shelley? Kelly? Kevin? Smelly? It was unreal. But I knew the girl in front of me was real. I knew I'd seen her somewhere before. But I didn't know where or when. And I didn't have a clue what she was doing.

Not that I had much time to think about it.

This Crazy Girl had stopped wobbling now. All of a sudden her legs sort of folded up and she fell over, head-first towards me. I didn't know what to do – but I knew I had to do *some*thing. I couldn't just stand there, could I? It's not every day you get the chance to catch a falling girl, is it? Even if she does look crazy.

So I dropped what I had in my hands, took a step forward, and grabbed the girl as she fell over.

She just slumped in my arms like a sack. She didn't move. She was leaning heavily on me, with her face slopped up against my chest. Her lipsticked mouth was dribbling onto my jacket. Now I really didn't know what to do. Where could I put my hands, for a start? On her back? Her head? Under her arms? Her waist? It was all a bit too intimate, if you know what I mean. Her body was right up next to mine, and her hands were squashed up against my legs ... and I couldn't help thinking that even if she did look a little bit crazy, she was also pretty hot.

Weird frizzy hair.

Thick gothy make-up.

Cool eyes.

Hot lips.

Tight jeans.

Nice legs.

OK, so she looked a bit of a mess at the moment. Maybe she was a bit plump, but that didn't bother me. It didn't bother me at all.

I *like* plump and messy.

Which is why I began to feel a bit awkward.

Then, to make things worse, she started slipping out of my arms and sliding down my body. Her lipstick left a bright red streak on my jacket. If I didn't get hold of her somewhere soon, we'd both end up even more embarrassed ...

So I grabbed hold of her. I picked her up under her arms. Then I kind of pulled her back up again. I thought I had a pretty good hold on her for a moment, but then I felt her slipping again so I had to move my hands fast to get a better grip ...

That's when her eyes suddenly opened.

"What the hell you *doing*?" she spat. She tried to get away from me. "Get your hands off me, you manky wee shite!"

I *think* that's what she said. She had a thick and angry Scottish accent. The words came rattling out of her mouth at the speed of light. She was still a bit dopey and dribbly too, so that didn't make her easy to understand. Furious + dribbly + Scottish = WHAT???? All I could hear was – *whitheheyeedoin? geyerhanzoffmee yeMANKYWEESHITE!*

I backed away from her and held up my hands. I tried to stay cool, and calm her down too. "I wasn't doing anything," I told her. "I was just—"

"Just what?" (*Jisswha?*)

"What?" I said. I couldn't understand what she'd just said.

"You were just what?"

"What?" I still couldn't understand.

She gave a sigh. "*You* said you weren't doing anything."

"I wasn't. I was just—" I went on.

"What? You were just what?" she shouted.

"I'm trying to *tell* you, but you keep—"

"I keep what?"

"—butting in,"

"Yeah?" she sneered. "Well, excuse *me* for butting in on your dirty wee groping session."

"I wasn't *groping* you."

"No?"

74

"You fainted," I told her.

That shut her up for a second. Her mouth went on moving but no words were coming out. I could see the anger slowly going away from her eyes. And she was starting to look a bit embarrassed, too.

"I *fainted?*" she said softly.

"Right into my arms," I grinned.

"Oh God," she muttered. "I fainted. I can't believe it. I *fainted* ..." And then she put her hand to her head and gave me a funny look. It was as if she'd suddenly remembered something else she'd done, something that made her feel even more embarrassed.

"Maybe it's the air in here," I told her. "It's too hot. I've been feeling a bit woozy too."

"What?"

"Woozy ... a bit dizzy," I said.

She looked at me for a long time then. She didn't say anything and she was thinking hard. I could almost hear her brain working.

In the end she said, "*You* don't remember, do you?"

"Remember what?" I asked.

"Nothing," she said, with a smile. "It's nothing. Forget it." She stepped up to me with her big smile and held out her hand. "I'm Sally," she said. "Sally Park. I'm a stylist."

"A *stylus*? What's that?" I frowned as I shook her hand.

"I'm a *stylist*," she said again, "stylist to the stars. Hey, look, I'm really sorry about all this, Kiefer. Y'know, like pure fainting all over you and everything ... then going all stroppy. God, you must think I'm a bampot."

"Not at all," I mumbled. *What was a bampot?* I thought.

The next thing I thought was that she'd called me Kiefer. And I remembered about the pass around my neck, the one that said *Kiefer Shelley*. I was back to feeling that I'd just woken up and I couldn't quite remember everything that had gone on. Slowly, I went over things in my head – the minibus, getting hit, falling down, getting hit again, falling down again ... and then something to do with the *Dead Holes* ...?

"What time are you on?" Sally said, breaking into my thoughts.

"What?"

She shook her head and said the question again, this time very slowly. She talked to me as if I didn't speak English. Or was stupid. Or both. "What ... time ... are ... you ... on?"

"On what?"

"On stage. What time are you playing?"

"Playing what?"

She grinned at me, and shook her head. "Don't start all that again—"

"Start what?" I said.

We looked at each other for a moment or two, and then we both started laughing like maniacs. I'm not sure if we knew *why* we were laughing, or even what we were laughing about, but somehow it didn't seem to matter.

We were just laughing.

And it felt pretty good.

Keith Scully

Spinning Around

After we'd stopped laughing, we got ourselves some food and a couple of bottles of beer and took it all over to a little table at the back of the tent. Sally had about three tons of food on one tiny plate. She was limping up and down on a broken heel, as she walked across to the table, and bits of meat and salad kept falling off her plate and dropping onto the floor.

As soon as we sat down, Sally started shovelling great handfuls of cake and kebab into her mouth. I couldn't help looking at her.

"Fwhaa?" she said.

"Nothing," I said, with a polite smile.

"I'm starving," she told me. "That's why I fainted."

She went on shovelling food into her mouth as fast as she could.

I picked at some nibbles and looked around the tent. It was hot and dark and thick with cigar smoke. There were lots of fat men in fat suits, and a few thin women in thin suits. They were all talking VERY LOUDLY – *OH YAH ... ABSOLUTELY ... HAH HAH ... YAH OH YAH ... BLAH BLAH ... BLAH BLAH BLAH.* Every now and then, one of them would look over at me, pretend to smile, then look away again.

In the background, I could just about hear the sounds of the *Dead Holes* blasting out their latest single – *You Kill Me*.

I was still puzzled about what had happened to me. Then slowly I began to remember – falling down the bank, taking Kiefer's pass, getting to the festival ... and then something must have happened which knocked me out for a while ...

And now here I was – in a big, dark tent with a crazy girl called Sally Park. But I liked her.

I looked at her again. She was still eating – curry and chocolate – but she'd slowed down a bit now. She had her eyes closed. She was thinking about her food, so I could have a really good look at her.

She had one of those odd faces that isn't beautiful or pretty, but still looks really good. The more I stared at it, the better it looked. In fact, everything about her looked really good. Her face, her figure, her dyed frizzy hair. She was wearing a really cool T-shirt too, a kind of raggedy cut-up thing made from the logos of ancient punk bands. Very cool … and *very* tight.

"D'you like it?"

I looked up quickly. I must have been staring a bit *too* hard. I could feel my face blushing.

"The T-shirt, I mean," Sally said, as she brushed some crumbs from her face.

"Oh yeah … yeah, it's great."

"It's one of mine."

"One of your what?"

She gave a smile. "I made it. I told you, I'm a stylist. Y'know – clothes and everything?"

"Oh, right," I said. "A *styli*st."

"That's what I said."

"You made *that*?" I asked her, and I nodded at her T-shirt.

"Yeah." She opened up her denim jacket so I could have a better look. "My favourite bands," she said. "*Pistols*, *Ramones* ... they could teach this lot a thing or two."

By this lot, she meant the *Dead Holes*. I could still hear them crashing away in the background.

"Christ," said Sally. "That lot are so bad, it's almost funny. I mean, *Anthem for Hate*? Don't make me laugh. What've *they* got to hate? Their minted mammies and daddies? Their big posh houses? Their fancy bloody cars?" She looked at me. She stopped. Then she said, "You don't *really* like them, do you?"

I didn't know what to say to that. I just looked at her, my mouth open and my brain spinning around in circles. Questions. Answers. Questions. Answers. Questions.

Q. If she thinks I'm Kiefer Shelley, why is she asking me if I like the *Dead Holes*?

A. Maybe she doesn't know who Kiefer is?

Q. So how come she knows that I like the *Dead Holes*?

A. Maybe I told her when I was knocked out?

Q. All right. What about all these other people in here? All these fat men and skinny women who keep looking at me? Do they think I'm Kiefer? Then who do they think's playing guitar with the *Dead Holes* right now?

A. Listen ... does that sound like Kiefer's guitar?

Q. No ... it doesn't. That's not Kiefer. That's someone else playing the guitar. What's all that about?

A. *God knows.*

"Kiefer?"

I blinked and looked across the table at Sally.

"You all right?" she asked me. She looked worried.

"Yeah, sorry … I'm fine. My head feels a bit funny, you know? I keep getting a bit dizzy." I looked at her. "I feel like I don't know what I'm doing half the time."

"Right …" she said. She looked at me again and nodded as if what I'd just said made some kind of sense. I still didn't know *why* it made sense …

But Sally seemed to understand.

"So," she went on with another smile, "d'you think you'll be OK to perform?"

"Perform?"

"Y'know … whatever you do …" She looked a bit shy. "Sorry, I don't actually *know* what you do. I mean, I know I should … it's just that I'm not really up on a lot of the new stuff. I kind of prefer all the old bands."

"Yeah," I said. "Me too."

"Really?"

"Yeah." I looked quickly at her T-shirt to get some names and ideas. "*Blondie*, *The Crash*, the *New York Rolls*—"

She started to laugh.

"What?" I said.

"It's *Dolls* – *New York Dolls*. And it's not *The Crash*, it's *The Clash*."

"Yeah," I muttered, "I *know* that. I was just—"

"Just what?"

I looked at her. She wasn't laughing in a nasty way, and she wasn't taking the piss. She didn't want to make me feel bad. She was just having a laugh with me – and it felt OK.

"That was a lie," I told her, with a sheepish grin. "In fact, I've never even heard of most of those bands."

"I kind of knew that."

I gave a shrug and grinned again.

She smiled and popped a tomato in her mouth.

We looked at each other.

I'd never felt better in all my life.

Sally stopped asking me tricky questions after that. What was she up to now? Why? She started talking about stuff that wasn't *all* about Kiefer. It was just stuff, you know – music, clothes, TV, people. It wasn't the most exciting talk – in fact, I can't even remember most of it – but at least it felt real.

And that was the problem – what was real and what wasn't ...

I was really starting to like Sally Park now, and I got the feeling that she kind of liked me too. But the thing was – I didn't know which *me* she liked.

Did she like me because I was Kiefer?

Or did she like me because I was me?

If she liked me because I was me, that was fine. But I'd only know that if I told her the truth. And if I told her the truth, and it turned out she only liked me because I was Kiefer, then there was a pretty good chance I'd end up stuck on my own again ... feeling fed up ... feeling crap ...

Feeling like Keith.

Do you see what I mean?

I didn't want to be Kiefer, but I didn't want to feel like Keith.

So what should I do?

I was still trying to come up with an answer when suddenly Sally stopped talking and was staring over my shoulder. Her mouth was open, her eyes enormous.

"Oh shit," she whispered.

I turned around and saw a big blond guy with a stupid, wavy haircut standing behind me. He was leaning forward and he was looking at the pass around Sally's neck. He had a pass around his neck, too.

BAND SECURITY, it said.

CRISPIN PARK, it said.

ACCESS ALL AREAS, it said.

Crispin? I thought.

Crispin *Park*?

As in Sally Park?

I turned back to Sally to ask her who he was. But before I could say anything my heart stopped beating and the words stuck in my throat. There was someone standing behind Sally too … someone looking at the pass around *my* neck. Someone in a white leather jacket.

"Oh shit," I croaked.

"Hey, Kiefer," grinned the real Kiefer. "Nice to meet you at last."

Sally Mack
Feeling the Frizzle

Typical Sally Mack bad luck.

Yeah. Should have known it was all too good to be true.

Me and Kiefer Shelley getting it together ...

We're in a dark corner of the VIP tent.

Necking free beer. Talking.

Looking right into each other's eyes.

Making each other laugh.

We've kinda drawn close so our arms are touching. You know when that happens with someone sometimes?

You don't know how, or when, or why?

But it's OK anyway.

Better than OK. Way better.

Kiefer's soft white jacket's rubbing against my T-shirt sleeve. Brushing the hairs on my arm. I smell the good leather mixed with the smell of him. Shampoo, gel, deodorant and a wee bit of sweat. And it's all just ...

Well, just dead *nice*, to use a crap word.

But it was just *nice*.

And sexy.

Kiefer's leg is pressing against mine. And he's warm. I'm comfy with Kiefer, whoever the hell he is. *Even* if he's some Custed Dusted McDie pin-up. I'm feeling all that VIP grub and bevvy hit the right spot. Feeling *really* good. Good-looking even. Because – and don't laugh – but I'm getting this *vibe* off Kiefer Shelley. See, I'm yakking on to him about the crap caff.

Auntie Rena.

How I *love* making T-shirts.

How I can't *live* without my favourite music.

How Kiefer's just gotta get himself into the sounds I like before it's too late …

And he's listening.

Saying, *Yeah, Sally. Maybe you'll burn me some tracks, Sally. That would be great, Sally …*

I'm wishing now I hadn't told him any extra stuff. Those *lies* about being a big-shot stylist. Because Kiefer's smiling into my eyes. Not bored. He keeps on and on just looking at me through his lovely, long eyelashes. Even when I burp. And I know, sure as I know I'm no Stylist to the Stars that Kiefer Shelley likes me for *me*. And I'm thinking –

*Sally Mack, if this cute guy doesn't jump on you quick, you're gonna have to throw yourself on top of him again. And this time he **will** get the Kiss of Life …*

There's a *frizzle* going on all over my body.

You *know* what I'm talking about.

The hairs at the nape of my neck are tingling. Me and Kiefer, our heads are nearly touching. We're at that *epic* moment. The first bit, the best bit of getting it together with someone.

When time slows down. You're gonna kiss.

And nothing. *Nothing* in the galaxy can stop it ...

Sally Mack
Meltdown

Nothing can stop that first kiss ... Unless your name's bloody Sally Mack.

And some big blond bruiser bloke yanks you to your feet with your ACCESS ALL AREAS Pass.

"Excuse me," blond bruiser bloke snorts. "Can I have a word?"

I gulp.

See I know fine who big blond bruiser is. I don't even have to check the name on his pass. His snooty voice is braying down into his walkie-talkie now.

"Security alert here, yah. Just kids, yah ..."

Then he holds back all this floppy, fair hair to look me up and down like I'm vomit on a stick. It's just the same look his sister threw me this morning.

Yeah.

Crispin Park might have tree trunk arms, a rugger-bugger neck and body-pump bumps rippling his ROCK STEADY T-shirt, but there's no way he can hide that he's from the same posh family as Rucksack Sally.

"You're not Sally Park. That's my sister's pass. And that's her jacket. And that's my Scouts rucksack. You dirty thief!" Crispin bellows into my face.

Bloody hell! The only decent thing about his voice is that it drowns out that crap band that's howling their *Anthem for Hate* song again. Crispin's shouting so loud that every fat and thin suit in the VIP tent turns round to stare. Glare. Tut. I hear myself try to answer back –

"Oi. I nicked nothin', mate. Yer sister threw her bloody bag at me. Lost me my friggin' job ..." Crispin's standing bang in front of me now so I have to peek round him to see what Kiefer's making of all this. Did he hear that posh twat Crispin sneering, "You're not Sally Park" to the whole of frigging *Rock Out*?

Help! I'm thinking. *What'll Kiefer do when he finds out I'm as fake as Michael Jackson's nose?*

I swing round Crispin to speak to Kiefer. I need to explain.

But Kiefer's not even looking at me.

"Shit," he's saying. "Oh shit."

He's looking through Crispin like he's seen a ghost.

"Kiefer ..." I begin again but Crispin moves in front. He grips the ACCESS ALL AREAS Pass round my neck.

"Out!" Crispin says, and he tugs at me. I'm choking, he's pulling the pass so hard. I swivel myself round to work free of the

pass. I duck down so it slips over my head ...
And there's Kiefer again.

For one snap second it looks like Kiefer's there. I can see the bright white leather jacket. The sticky-up hair.

But this guy doesn't have ripped jeans on. Nah.

We're talking about a different guy altogether here.

Taller. Older. Uglier.

He's carrying a guitar shaped like a gun.

Tragic or what? I'm thinking. *What a sad guitar.*

"Nice to meet you at last," the new Kiefer says slowly to my Kiefer. He thuds his hands down on my Kiefer's shoulders and pins him to the spot. He sounds even more pissed off than Crispin. And his voice is even posher.

"What you playing at, dude?" posh Kiefer yells at my Kiefer like he's dirt. "I quit the band for ten minutes and you jump in. Steal my gear. We had to 'copter me in another jacket from Milan. You didn't really think you'd get away with it, kid, did you?" Posh Kiefer says with a nasty sneer.

He's looking at my Kiefer the way Crispin looked at me. Except my Kiefer's not really Kiefer, is he?

"OK. OK. I'm Keith Scully," my Kiefer grunts as Kiefer Shelley rams the gun-shaped guitar into Keith's goolies.

"That's better," Kiefer Shelley smirks. "So why are you dressed up like a *Dead Hole*, Keith Scully?"

"'Cos you chucked all this stuff away," Keith groans.

Keith Scully's looking at me, not Kiefer Shelley, when he says this. Maybe because I'm the only one who bothers to listen to him. The real Kiefer Shelley doesn't.

"Shut up, shut up, shut UP," Kiefer Shelley shouts into Keith's face. "D'you know I've thousands of fans dying for me out there, man? But I can't get on stage to do my thing 'cos some skinny kid's wearing this," Kiefer Shelley yells. He tugs the ACCESS ALL AREAS Pass over Keith's head. Then Kiefer Shelley uses his guitar to jab Keith out the VIP tent.

There's a wall of ROCK STEADY giants standing out there. Arms folded.

"He's all yours," Kiefer Shelley sneers.

Then he's off. He flounces to the nearest stage with his guitar high in the air.

I can hear him on stage now. "Hel-lo, *Rock Out*. How you doin'?" Kiefer Shelley bawls in a cockney accent.

A MASSIVE cheer goes up outside the VIP tent, but I can't see what's going on. Can't see the stage. Can't even see Keith Scully. Just Crispin Park. He's pulling at my T-shirt. He grabs my rucksack.

"That's mine!" he says but I just hold onto it tighter. He's not getting that rucksack back. I kick it out of his reach. So he grabs my arm instead. Pulls it up behind my back.

"Out, thief," Crispin brays. Bloody hell! He's hurting me. I fight until he has to let me go. Before he grabs me again I pick up Kiefer's holdall and the rucksack and batter Crispin off with them both.

"Don't mess with me, pal," I say. Then, all of a sudden, this HORRIBLE noise starts flooding the air. Someone is HOWLING. Sounds like some poor guy's getting a huge electric shock.

I know who that person is. Kiefer Shelley must be up on stage now. Oh dear, I think I hear him wailing about goblins. I bet his legs are wide enough apart to split his trousers and he'll be jerking his crotch about, like something's biting him down under. He'll be playing his gun-guitar above his head. Upside down.

"What a twat. Those *Dead Holes* suck," I say out loud. If I wasn't carrying both bags and trying to get away from Crispin, I might laugh too.

But none of this is funny.

And it was no joke being run out of *Rock Out* on a broken heel. Plus I'm carrying a lumpy great rucksack and a heavy holdall. And all I want is to stop and find someone. Make sure he's OK.

I can't see Keith Scully anywhere. He isn't outside the VIP tent. But that's where the white leather jacket is. It's on the ground.

Bloody.

Trampled.

Like road kill.

I feel sick when I see it. I feel even sicker when I'm outside the gates of *Rock Out*. I sit down on the rucksack and hug Keith's holdall.

"Where are you, Keith?" I whisper. I unzip the bag. What are the chances of him being hidden inside? Instead there's a tatty white jacket. It's all patches and studs and badges and it stinks of cow shit. I hold it tight against my T-shirt.

Keith Scully

The Best Thing
in the World

You know what it's like when you've spent all your life feeling like crap and then someone comes along and makes you feel good? You know how that feels? It feels like the best thing in the world. Like nothing else matters. Nothing at all. Like there *is* nothing else. There's just YOU and your SOMEONE ELSE, and that's it.

Nothing else matters.

That's how it was. When Kiefer punched me with his guitar where it hurts and ripped his Backstage Pass off my neck – it didn't matter. When the ROCK STEADY guys shoved me out of the VIP tent and marched me along through hundreds of screaming *Dead Holes* fans – it didn't matter. When they dragged me over to the gates and kicked me out – it didn't matter. When I pulled off Kiefer's jacket and chucked it on the ground and then turned around and gave the ROCK STEADY guys the finger – it didn't matter. But then one of them suddenly came after me, lumbering through the mud at 100 mph, like a mad rhino ...

Yeah, well that *did* matter.

But not for long.

I legged it into a giant field full of millions of parked cars and the rhino soon gave up. I hid down behind a 4 X 4 and watched him slowly coming to a halt at the edge of the field. He stood there looking tough for a minute. He flexed his huge arms as he looked around the field, then he grunted something into his radio, turned round, and stomped back over to the gates.

My heart was beating hard.

My chest felt tight.

My legs shook.

I sat down and took some deep breaths.

"Shit," I said.

It was cow shit. And I was sitting in it. My nose was bleeding too. Kiefer must have whacked it when he yanked the pass over my head. I was bleeding all over the place and sitting in shit.

But, you know what?

It didn't matter.

All that mattered was Sally.

I was a *bit* worried about a few other things. Who was the real Sally? Why had the big blond guy said she was a thief? And what would she think about me pretending to be Kiefer Shelley? But when I stood up and looked over at the gates and saw the big blond guy throwing her out of the festival, I knew that none of it mattered.

Sally was fighting and shouting and cursing like a crazy thing. A beautiful crazy thing.

And when I saw her take my old white jacket out of the holdall and hug it, I nearly died.

The big ROCK STEADY guys were still hanging around the gates. If I shouted out to Sally they'd hear me, then they'd come after me again. If they caught me they'd most likely beat the crap out of me.

I thought about that for about one second, then I took a deep breath and shouted like hell.

"SALLY! HEY, SALLY!! I'M OVER HERE!!! SAAAAALLLLLLYYYY!!!!!"

The ROCK STEADY guys *did* hear me, but they didn't do anything about it. They were too busy looking cool and hard. They just stared at me for a moment, gave me the evil eye, then they turned to watch Sally. She was running over to me now. She was hopping and limping and pulling her bags behind her. The ROCK STEADY guys started to laugh. They were hooting at her as they shook their big, fat heads. But Sally didn't care. And nor did I.

I felt so good I thought I was going to explode.

I couldn't breathe.

My lungs were bursting.

My heart was swelling up like a hot-air balloon.

Sally was running ... she was *running*. She was running to me. To *me* – to Keith Scully. And she was smiling at me, too – a big, mad, crazy smile that lit up her face and made me go weak at the knees. She was running ... I just couldn't believe it. Running across the field, waving her hands. She dodged around the parked cars ... and just for a moment I thought I was dreaming again. It was the kind of dream where someone's running towards you ... but they never get to you. They just keep running and running and running forever, but they never get any closer ...

I started to think – *it's too good to be true. It's always too good to be true …*

But then suddenly she was there.

It wasn't a dream.

She was right there in front of me. She limped through the mud and dropped her bags on the ground. She was smiling and out of breath …

And then she grabbed me, hugged me hard and the next thing I knew we were down on the ground, kissing and hugging each other. We couldn't stop.

Whew! It makes me feel hot just thinking about it. And it *was* hot. We didn't say anything for about five minutes. We just held onto each other and rolled around – lips and tongues and warm bodies.

Nothing else mattered.

After a bit, we both sat up. Sally looked stunning. She was covered in mud and grass. Her hair was all over the place and her eyes were wild and bright. All I could do was stare at her.

"All right?" she asked, with a grin.

I nodded.

"I'm Sally Mack," she said.

"And I'm Keith Scully," I told her.

We shook hands. We were both smiling like mad.

Sally pulled a tissue out of her pocket and wiped some blood from my nose.

"Thanks," I said.

She smiled again. "Do you want to know who Sally Park is?"

"Not really. D'you want me to tell you about Kiefer Shelley?"

"Maybe later – come here."

She put her arms around me and we rolled back down onto the ground.

We didn't get around to talking to each other till later. As the sun began to go down, and the festival music drifted around in the crimson sky, we sat together in the car park and told each other our stories. Sally told me about the Last Stop Caff and Auntie Rena and how she became Sally Park for the day. I told her all about Danny and James and the train journey from hell and the bus to nowhere and how I'd been Kiefer Shelley for the day.

And it was all OK.

None of it mattered. It was nice just to sit there and talk about it. Watching the sun go down. Having a laugh. Listening to the music.

It was *nice*.

"It's a shame we're missing it all," Sally said, looking across towards the festival. "There's some really good bands on tonight."

"Hey," I said. I'd forgotten until that moment. "I've still got my *Rock Out* tickets – I didn't have to use them before."

"Yeah," she said, "but they won't let us back in, will they? Even if we *have* got tickets. They threw us out, remember? They know who we are. They're not going to let us back in again."

"Yeah, I suppose ..."

"Unless ..."

I looked at her. "Unless what?"

A mad grin cracked her face. She grabbed her huge rucksack and started digging around inside it. She started singing – *I see you baby ...* – wailing away like a lunatic as she pulled everything out of the rucksack and threw it on the ground. I couldn't believe what she had. There was half a department store in there – earplugs, Pot Noodles, a kettle, an iron, a giant-sized make-up bag, hair tongs, bog rolls, wet wipes, pyjamas, a sleeping bag, a pillow ... four lace thongs.

When she pulled out the thongs she looked at me and winked.

"Later, baby ..."

I blushed.

She laughed, then pulled off her T-shirt, making me blush even more.

"Here," she said, throwing me the T-shirt. "Put it on."

I looked at her, trying to stay cool. "Uhh ... what are you doing?"

"The guys on the gates," she said, "they know who we are, right? They know what we look like."

"Right."

"So they'll be watching out for a gorgeous boy in a white leather jacket and a frizzy-haired goth-girl in a super-funky T-shirt. Right?"

"Yeah ..."

She grinned. "They *won't* be looking out for a gorgeous goth-boy in a super-funky T-shirt and a straight-haired posh tart in a white leather jacket."

She looked at me. I smiled at her.

"Get your clothes off," she said. "And pass me those hair tongs."

Keith Scully
The Only Way to Be

Half an hour later we were walking through the gates together. We held hands and we were grinning like idiots. The night was hot and steamy and the festival was rocking. We could feel the music throbbing in the air. We felt good, we looked good. We looked totally different. The security guys didn't have a clue who we were.

"Piece of cake," I whispered to Sally as I handed over the tickets.

"Mmmm ..." she said, "... piece ... of ... cake ..."

She looked amazing. Straight hair, posh make-up, lip-gloss, tight jeans. She'd cleaned up my white leather jacket and removed all the badges. She was wearing it on top of a slinky little pyjama-top thing she'd found in the rucksack. She looked absolutely stunning. I couldn't keep my eyes off her.

And she couldn't keep her eyes off me.

She'd got me all made up with lipstick and mascara and big, spiky hair, and she'd ripped her funky T-shirt so it fitted me just right …

"You look fantastic," she told me as we headed for the stage.

"So do you," I said, ogling her again. "You look kind of different, but you're still you – if you know what I mean."

"You mean I don't look like Sally Park?"

"You never did."

"And you never looked like Kiefer Shelley, either – thank God."

I looked at her. "What do you think would have happened if we hadn't found out? I mean, if I still thought you were Sally Park and you still thought I was Kiefer. What do you think we'd be doing now?"

She stopped and looked at me. Her eyes were as bright as the moon. "I don't know what we'd be doing right now," she said, "but I'm pretty sure that Sally and Kiefer wouldn't be doing what we're going to be doing later on."

"Why?" I said stupidly. "What are we doing later on?"

She smiled at me, then leaned in close and whispered in my ear.

Her words turned me inside out.

I didn't know what to say back, so I didn't say anything. I just stood there, grinning like mad and trying to look cool. Sally grinned back at me for a moment. Then we kissed again, soft and sweet. She took me by the hand and dragged me off towards the stage.

We spent the rest of the night just being ourselves. And when the morning came we both knew it was the only way to be.

Barrington Stoke would like to thank all its readers for commenting on the manuscript before publication and in particular:

Philip Anderson

Michael Ashton

Ryan Bell

Jamie Booth

Mrs Catherine Brotherstone

Sean Robert Brunton

Murray Buchanan

Rebecca Burns

Natasha Burrell

Gregg Cameron

Dan Coia

Jane Coward

Jennifer Daly

Caeleigh Drummond

Mrs Flatts

Abby Ford

Kevin Fortune

Jordan Harley

Connor Henderson

Mrs Margaret Hutchinson

Phoebe Janner

Steven Jones

Mrs Janet Leifer

Nicky Mackay

Eleanor Morton

Emmanuel Neizer

Zara Raiker

Annie Rayner

Hynde Ritchie

Katie Riva

Daniel Sanders

Evelyn Smith

Amanda Swift

Amanda Wallace

Become a Consultant!

Would you like to give us feedback on our titles before they are published? Contact us at the email address below – we'd love to hear from you!

info@barringtonstoke.co.uk
www.barringtonstoke.co.uk

Meet the Authors ...

What's the best thing about writing with someone else?

KB I've never written with anyone else before, so it was really exciting (and a little bit scary!) to write this book with Cathy. The best bit for me was sharing all the stuff that makes writing a book so special – the ideas, the problems, the surprises, the excitement, and – most of all – the wonder of where it all comes from.

And the worst?

KB Letting another writer see what you're writing – it's terrifying!

CF Having to wait for the next bit of the story to come from Kev when I was desperate to know what happened next and tempted just to carry on writing it myself.

How do you normally write a book?

CF I normally write a book and keep on going until it's finished. I never, ever discuss it with anyone until I've written a first draft, or show anyone any of it. (Basically because I think everything I write is drivel till it's finished.)

How is writing with someone else different?

CF Writing with Kev meant he was looking at the drivel – I mean story – a chapter at a time.

How did you write together? In person, by phone, email?

KB A mixture of all three, really. We started off by meeting up a few times and working out what the basic story was going to be, then we started writing separately but kept in touch by phone and email, sending each other what we'd done, discussing it, changing it, updating it, and so on.

Any gossip/arguments we should know about?

KB None at all – honestly! We get on really well, and we have very similar approaches, both to writing and life in general. And, besides, we're both too nice to have arguments. Well, Cathy is ... I'm just too weedy.

Did it turn out like you thought it would?

KB Yes and no. I think we both knew what kind of story we wanted to write, and we were both fairly confident we could do something together, but when we started writing, and the characters started coming to life, that was simply amazing. The story took on a life of its own, and the characters just seemed to grow with each other, almost beyond our control, and by the end of the book I think we both knew that the story belonged to Keith and Sally – not us. And that was fantastic.

Why did you decide to work together?

CF We didn't decide to work together. Anna Gibbons at Barrington Stoke forced us to do it and we were too scared of her to say no!

Do you prefer working together or on your own?

KB I'm sure that Cathy – and every other writer in the world – would probably agree that writing books is essentially something you do on your own. Once a story has been written and published, it then becomes something to be shared by everyone, but the actual process of writing a book is a very personal and private thing. So, although I really enjoyed working with Cathy on this book – and I'd be delighted to do it again some time – I'd have to say that I still prefer writing on my own. I'd also have to say that this is a very unfair question!

CF Yes is the short answer although, saying that, I would love to write with Kev again having done it. I'm really pleased with the way *I See You Baby ...* worked out and I love the happy ending Kev wrote. I don't think I could write the same way with anyone else. He's a top guy!